THE START OF SOMETHING BIG

A HOT AIR BALLOON ADVENTURE STORY

ANNAHITA DE LA MARE & JENNIFER KIRKHAM

It was a beautiful day, and three cousins were playing hide and seek in the garden.

"...18...19...20, coming ready or not!" called Alice.

A giggle from behind the next tree gave away Hannah's hiding place, but where was Rosie?

"Found you!" called Alice and Hannah as they burst into the shed.

"Look what I found!" shouted Rosie. "Do you remember Grandma telling us about her hot air balloon adventures? This must be her balloon!" The fabric was torn, the basket had holes and the door was hanging on a hinge. But it was definitely a hot air balloon!

"Grandma **is** expecting us for dinner..." said Alice. "And the bus is **always** late..." added Hannah. A flicker of excitement passed between them.

They rummaged through the shed for the tools they would need, then set to work.

Once the repairs were complete, the balloon was fit to fly.
"Are we **really** going to do this?" asked Rosie nervously.
"Oh yes!" said Alice with a grin.

They all piled in and Alice flicked a switch to light the burner.
Slowly, but surely, the balloon rose into the air.
"We're off! It worked!" Alice squealed.

Uh oh...

Extracting the balloon from the tree was not an easy task.
Nor was extracting the tree from their hair.
Luckily, Roger the cat was at hand to help.

"We should have checked the wind direction before take-off," said Hannah.

"Or taken the bus. We still could?" suggested Rosie hopefully.

"We always take the bus!" replied Alice. "This is way more exciting. Come on, let's try again."

The girls piled in for another go. Roger wasn't so brave, he sauntered off for a sleep instead.

This time, they soared gracefully into the air.
"We did it!" exclaimed Hannah, "Grandma always
says: if you put your minds to something, and you put
your heads together; you can do anything."
"She is going to be SO proud!" said Alice.

"We need to get over this bridge first!" cried Rosie nervously.

"Or under it!" dared Alice. She yanked on a cord to open an air flap
at the top of the balloon.

Hot air rushed out. The balloon lurched...

...and swung precariously under the tunnel.

"Phew, that was close!" breathed Hannah in relief.
"Let's try to stay a bit higher, shall we?"

"**STARTING RIGHT NOW?**" shouted Rosie, as they shot towards a pair of very tall buildings.

Alice threw the burners up to full flow and the balloon rose just in time; the basket skimming gracefully through the narrow gap.

The girls breathed a collective sigh of relief as they headed away from the city centre.

"There goes the bus..." muttered Rosie wistfully.
A gentle breeze tickled their hair. The hot sun warmed their cheeks.
The balloon's burners puffed like a friendly old dragon. Alice, Hannah
and Rosie's smiles slowly returned as they drifted
peacefully towards Grandma's.

As they approached, Grandma and Gordon
the horse looked up in surprise.
"My old balloon! You fixed it!" cried Grandma,
clapping her hands in delight.
"Oh you clever girls, I always said if you put your minds to
something, and you put your heads together…"

"We can do **anything!**" finished the girls.

"We did have a few close shaves on the way…" admitted Hannah.

"And an incident with a tree…" added Rosie.

"Nothing goes smoothly on the first try, girls!" said Grandma. "Learning a new skill takes time. But it's **always** worth it in the end. Come. You must be hungry after your adventure!"

Grandma's fridge was a thing of magic. Whenever Grandma poked her head in, she would come out minutes later laden with enough food to feed a whole school of children. Which was lucky, because the girls really were famished. So was Gordon.

After dinner, Grandma couldn't wait to join her grandchildren for a ride.
"Um, is Gordon coming too?" asked Hannah.
"Of course, I'll need a ride back home," replied Grandma.
She gave Gordon a gentle shove, sending him shuffling into the balloon.

It was difficult taking off with all the extra weight, but they managed.

Rosie took control of the burners as they neared the city, sending them
high up into the sky, far above the buildings and bridges.
"Excellent flying, girls!" exclaimed Grandma.
The girls grinned with pride.

"You know though, when you fly above a certain height, the winds turn to the right. It's called the Coriolis effect," said Grandma.

"Oh. But Hannah's house is over to the left," said Alice.

"So then we need to go lower again," added Hannah.

Grandma nodded.

"How low..?" asked Rosie nervously.

Grandma's eyes twinkled with mischief. She leaned over the basket and

...**spat**.

"GRANDMA! That's disgusting!" exclaimed the girls through hoots of laughter.
"True. But look! **There!**" The girls looked. "The spit changed direction. If you lower the balloon down to that point, we will turn left."
The girls were impressed. The bird was not. Rosie opened the air flap a fraction, allowing them to gently descend to the correct level.

Grandma sighed happily. It was wonderful to be back in the hot air balloon. "My darlings," she said with a knowing smile. "I have a feeling this is the start of something big for you…"

Gordon snorted. "Now now Gordon," chided Grandma. "Hot air ballooning is a wonderful way to explore the world!"
Gordon whinnied unhappily. "Don't worry my love, **my** adventuring days are long since passed."
Relieved, Gordon nuzzled Grandma's neck.
Grandma chuckled and patted his nose affectionately.

They landed smoothly and packed the balloon away for another day. It was late and the girls were tired.

After cleaning their teeth, the girls settled into Hannah's room for a sleepover.

"You were right Alice," said Rosie. "That was **so** much better than the bus! I can't wait to fly again!"
"Me neither!" said Alice, "Where shall we go next? I have a few ideas..."

Before long, they had run out of paper to write on, and their eyelids were drooping with tiredness.

Rosie turned out the light and the three cousins fell into a deep, contented sleep.
Their dreams were filled with white snowy mountains, sparkling blue seas and pastel green savannahs. What adventures they were going to have in their hot air balloon!

For Olivia, Emilia, Emily and Hannah: because cousins rule!

First published in 2018 by MDLM Books
Schönenberg, Switzerland
www.mdlmbooks.com
Follow us on Instagram, Facebook and Twitter @mdlmbooks

ISBN (Hardback): 978-3-9525029-0-7
ISBN (Paperback): 978-3-9525029-1-4

British Library Cataloguing-in-Publication Data
A catalogue record for this book is available from the British Library.

In 'The Perfect Rainy Day', the girls encounter graceful giraffes, farting zebras and roaring lions on a brilliant hot air balloon adventure to Africa!

In 'Footprints in the Snow' the cousins fly to Iceland for a spot of springtime snowboarding, and end up on the trial of an abominable snowman!

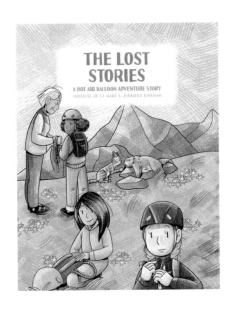

In 'The Lost Stories' the girls, Roger and Grandma tackle the treacherous north face of the Eiger in search of a long lost treasure!

Made in the USA
Middletown, DE
23 November 2020